Dentist Trip

Every morning, Peppa and George brush their teeth. Scrub! Scrub! Scrub!

"You both have lovely clean teeth. I'm sure the dentist will be happy!" calls out Daddy Pig.

Later that day, Peppa and George are at the dentists, waiting for their check-up. It is George's first visit.

"Peppa! George! The dentist will see you now!" says Miss Rabbit, the nurse. "Hooray!" they both cheer.

This is Doctor Elephant, the dentist. "Who's first?" he asks.

"I'm first," replies Peppa. "I'm a big girl. Watch me, George!"

"Open wide, please!" orders
Doctor Elephant, softly.
"Aaaaah . . ." Peppa opens her mouth
as wide as she possibly can.
"Let's take a look!" says the dentist,
checking Peppa's teeth with a mirror.

"There. All done! What lovely clean teeth!" cheers Doctor Elephant. "Now, you can have the special drink." Gargle! Ptooou! Peppa spits the pink liquid out into the sink. It's George's turn next.

George does not want it to be his turn. So the dentist lets him hold Mr Dinosaur. "All done. You have very strong, clean teeth, George!" smiles Doctor Elephant.

"But wait, what is this?" cries Doctor Elephant. "George has clean teeth, but this young dinosaur's teeth are very dirty."

"Pink!" cries George, picking up a glass. "That's right, George!" says the dentist. "Mr Dinosaur needs some special pink drink!" Gurgle! Gurgle!